Welcome to The Giggle Club

The Giggle Club is a collection of new picture books made to put a giggle into early reading. There are funny stories about a contrary mouse, a dancing fox, a turtle with a trumpet, a pig with a ball, a hungry monster, a laughing lobster, an elephant who sneezes away the jungle and lots more! Each of these characters is a member of **The Giggle Club**, but anyone can join: just pick up a **Giggle Club** book, read it and get giggling!

Turn to the checklist on the inside back cover and tick off the Giggle Club books you have read.

TEE HEE!

HA HA!

For Linda

First published 1996 by Walker Books Ltd
87 Vauxhall Walk, London SE11 5HJ

This edition published 1997

10 9 8 7 6 5 4 3 2

© 1996 Alan Baron

This book has been typeset in Veronan.

Printed in Hong Kong

British Library Cataloguing in Publication Data
A catalogue record for this book is
available from the British Library.

ISBN 0-7445-5281-8

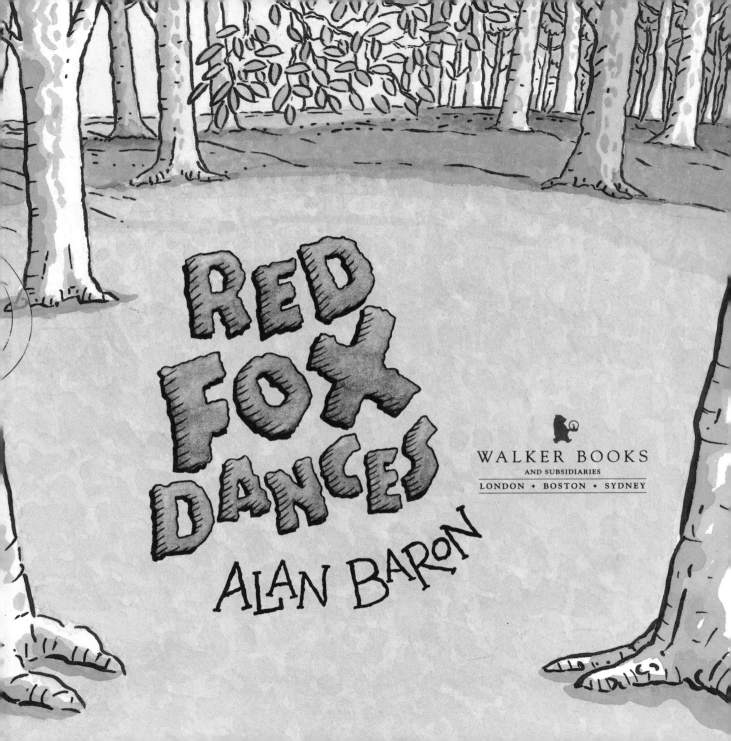

RED FOX DANCES

ALAN BARON

WALKER BOOKS
AND SUBSIDIARIES
LONDON · BOSTON · SYDNEY

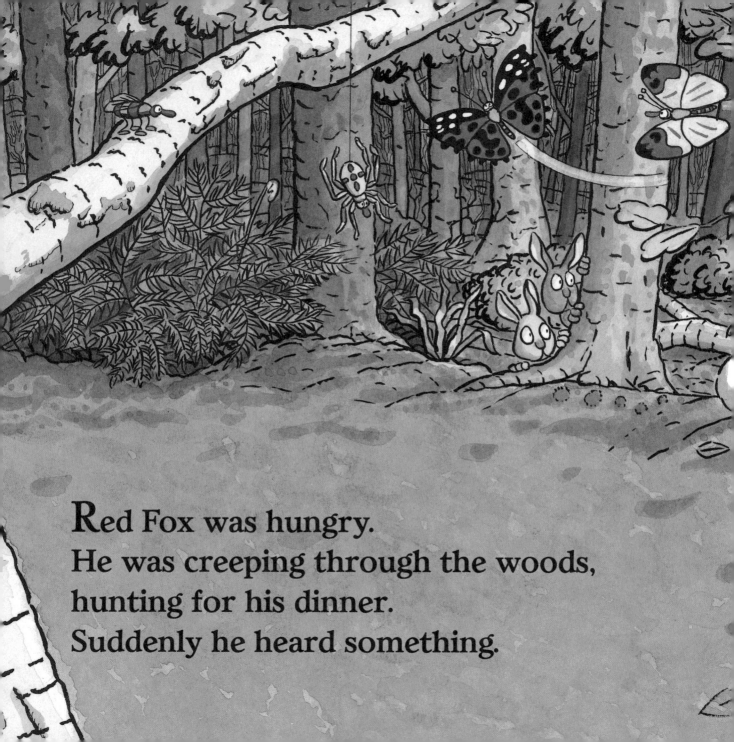

Red Fox was hungry.
He was creeping through the woods,
hunting for his dinner.
Suddenly he heard something.

Red Fox crept towards the sound.
He crouched behind a bush.
He saw Little Pig dancing a jig.
Ah, dinner! Red Fox licked his lips.
But Dan Dog was there too,
playing the fiddle.
Red Fox watched and waited.

Along came
Big Duck and Fat Hen.
They began to dance a jig.
Little Pig hopped and bopped.
Dan Dog played faster.
Behind the bush, Red Fox began
to tap his toes.

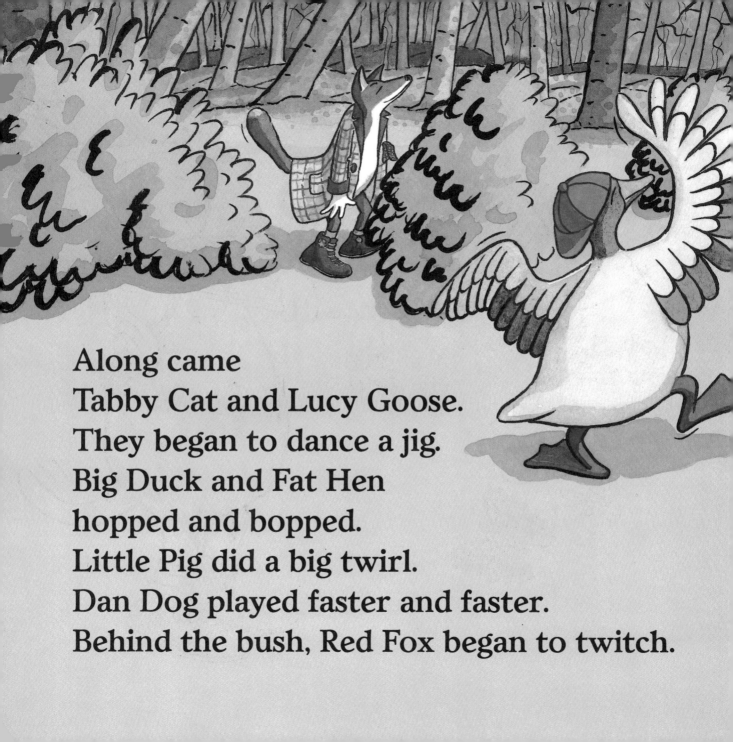

Along came
Tabby Cat and Lucy Goose.
They began to dance a jig.
Big Duck and Fat Hen
hopped and bopped.
Little Pig did a big twirl.
Dan Dog played faster and faster.
Behind the bush, Red Fox began to twitch.

Suddenly Red Fox
jumped out.
"Call that dancing?"
he shouted. "I'll show you how to dance!"
Everyone was terribly frightened.
But Dan Dog kept playing
so everyone kept dancing.

Red Fox started to dance.

He rocked and rolled.

He skipped and jumped.

He did high kicks and big leaps.

He bounced and bounced and bounced.

Red Fox was so busy showing off
he didn't notice everyone was
dancing away from him.
He didn't notice the music
growing fainter and fainter.

Suddenly Red Fox
remembered he was hungry.
He stopped dancing and looked around.
"WHERE'S MY DINNER?" he howled.
But there was no answer.
Red Fox's dinner had danced away.

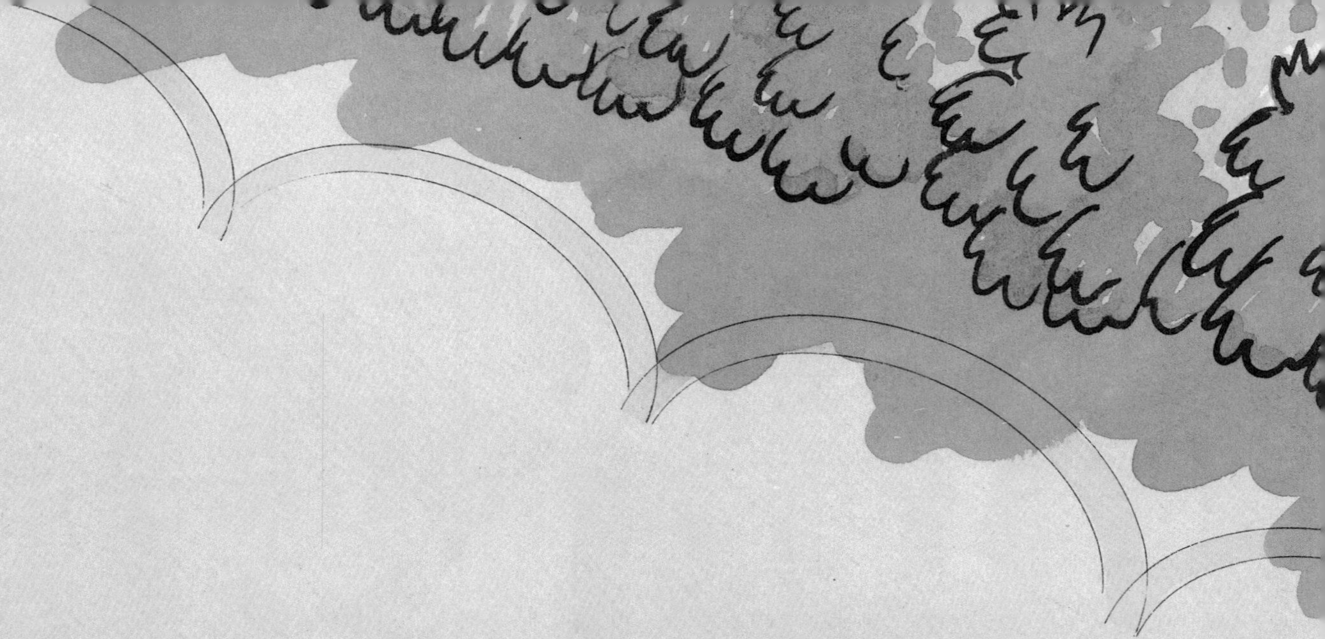